W9-BTA-598

AVENGERS K #3

ASSEMBLING THE AVENGERS

Tasked by the World Security Council with unlocking the mysteries of the Tesseract, S.H.I.E.L.D. Director Nick Fury finds his attention divided. Tony Stark has only 72 hours left before the arc reactor in his chest kills him, but no viable cure yet exists. Meanwhile, strange weather patterns in New Mexico have led Agent Phil Coulson to the conclusion that something big is on the horizon.

JIM ZUB
SCRIPT

WOO BIN CHOI WITH **JAE SUNG LEE**
ART

MIN JU LEE
INKS

JAE WOONG LEE, HEE YE CHO & IN YOUNG LEE
COLORS

VC's CORY PETIT
LETTERS

WOO BIN CHOI WITH **JAE SUNG LEE, MIN JU LEE, JAE WOONG LEE & HEE YE CHO**
COVER ART

Adapted from MARVEL'S AVENGERS PRELUDE: FURY'S BIG WEEK #1-4.
Adaptations written by SI YEON PARK and translated by JI EUN PARK

AVENGERS created by STAN LEE and JACK KIRBY

Original comics written by CHRIS YOST and ERIC PEARSON
and illustrated by LUKE ROSS DANIEL HDR AGUSTIN PADILLA DON HO
WELLINTON ALVES RICK KETCHAM MARK PENNINGTON and CHRIS SOTOMAYOR

Editor: SARAH BRUNSTAD
Manager, Licensed Publishing: JEFF REINGOLD
VP, Brand Management & Development, Asia: C.B. CEBULSKI
VP Production & Special Projects: JEFF YOUNGQUIST
SVP Print, Sales & Marketing: DAVID GABRIEL
Associate Managing, Digital Assets: JOE HOCHSTEIN
Associate Managing Editor: KATERI WOODY
Assistant Editor: CAITLIN O'CONNELL
Senior Editor, Special Projects: JENNIFER GRÜNWALD
Editor, Special Projects: MARK D. BEAZLEY
Book Designer: ADAM DEL RE

Editor In Chief: AXEL ALONSO
Chief Creative Officer: JOE QUESADA
President: DAN BUCKLEY
Executive Producer: ALAN FINE

Spotlight

AVENGERS ACTIVE ROSTER

THOR
Real Name:
THOR ODINSON

IRON MAN
Real Name:
ANTHONY
EDWARD STARK

CAPTAIN AMERICA
Real Name: STEVEN ROGERS

HAWKEYE
Real Name:
CLINT
BARTON

BLACK WIDOW
Real Name:
NATASHA ROMANOFF

NICK FURY

HULK
Real Name:
ROBERT BRUCE BANNER

EXTRAORDINARY ALLIES

PHIL COULSON

WAR MACHINE

JANE FOSTER

AVENGERS MOST WANTED

WHIPLASH

LOKI

DESTROYER

ABOMINATION

SAMUEL STERNS

ABDOPUBLISHING.COM

Reinforced library bound edition published in 2018 by Spotlight, a division of ABDO, PO Box 398166, Minneapolis, Minnesota 55439. Spotlight produces high-quality reinforced library bound editions for schools and libraries. Published by agreement with Marvel Characters, Inc. Printed in the United States of America, North Mankato, Minnesota.
092017   012018

PUBLISHER'S CATALOGING-IN-PUBLICATION DATA

Names: Zub, Jim, author. | Choi, Woo Bin; Lee, Jae Sung; Lee, Min Ju; Lee, Jae Woong; Cho, Hee Ye; Lee, In Young, illustrators.
Title: Assembling the Avengers / writer: Jim Zub ; art: Woo Bin Choi; Jae Sung Lee; Min Ju Lee; Jae Woong Lee; Hee Ye Cho; In Young Lee.
Description: Minneapolis, MN : Spotlight, 2018 | Series: Avengers K Set 3
Summary: With a changing world full of threats bigger than he could imagine, S.H.I.E.L.D. director Nick Fury struggles to follow orders from the World Security Council. He calls upon Agent Coulson, Hawkeye, and Black Widow for aid to search for the missing Captain America, help Tony Stark fix his failing arc reactor in his chest, stop the Hulk from going on a rampage, and unearth an alien object, followed shortly by its electrifying owner.
Identifiers: LCCN 2017941923 | ISBN 9781532141478 (v.1 ; lib. bdg.) | ISBN 9781532141485 (v.2 ; lib. bdg.) | ISBN 9781532141492 (v.3 ; lib. bdg.) | ISBN 9781532141508 (v.4 ; lib. bdg.) | ISBN 9781532141515 (v.5 ; lib. bdg.) | ISBN 9781532141522 (v.6 ; lib. bdg.) | ISBN 9781532141539 (v.7 ; lib.bdg.)
Subjects: LCSH: Avengers (ficitious character)--Juvenile fiction. | Super heroes--Juvenile fiction. | Graphic Novels--Juvenile fiction. | Media Tie-in--Juvenile fiction.
Classification: DDC 741.5--dc23
LC record available at http://lccn.loc.gov/2017941923

ABDO
Spotlight

A Division of ABDO
abdopublishing.com

"IRON MAN:
OUT OF CONTROL"

PART 2

OKAY. I THINK THAT WARRANTS MY ATTENTION.

WHO'S THAT? I DON'T RECOGNIZE HER.

THAT'S *JANE FOSTER*, AN ASTROPHYSICIST. SHE DETECTED THE SAME ACTIVITY AND HAS BEEN STUDYING IT FOR WEEKS NOW.

CONGRATULATIONS, YOU JUST GOT REASSIGNED. GO CHECK IT OUT.

WHOA!

IS IRON MAN... DEAD?

WOOOSH

ALL RIGHT!

AMAZING! HE'S UNSTOPPABLE!

TH-THANK YOU.

NATASHA, GIVE ME AN UPDATE.

TO BE CONTINUED!